Pricilla Parsnip

The Tails of Many Tales
From
the Land of Barely There

by

Stephen E. Cosgrove

Illustrated by

Wendy Edelson

DreamMaker

111 Avenida Palizada West
San Clemente, CA 92672

The Tails of Many Tales
From
The Land of Barely There

Dedicated to Nancy, my wife of lo these many years. When I was down she encouraged and enlightened without drenching the advice in caramel or cream; at times a bitter pill, indeed. But from that bitter pill I got better just the same. Truly a better bitter pill. I love you!

Stephen

About web-enhanced SakesAlive Books

This is one of many stories from the land of Barely There. Like all stories it contains a beginning a middle and an end. Unlike other stories you have read the story continues on the internet at a site called SakesAlive™:

http://www.sakesalive.com

When you have finished reading Pricilla Parsnip visit SakesAlive and continue your adventure by writing letters to the characters in this book.
If you write them they will answer you in kind with a very unique and very special e-mail from SakesAlive.

My oh my, SakesAlive
characters are living
and here they thrive.
My, oh my, SakesAlive!

sakesalive.com

arther than far and to the very edge of the horizon was a path bordered in lacy fern. If you followed that path on a rainy day, skipping across puddles and the like, you would find the Land of Barely There.

Barely There... where songbirds sing to any and all that will listen.

Barely There... where anything and every-thing can happen and often does.

If you followed that path as it wandered
past Hideaway Glen and through the
Whispering Forest you would soon find your-
self in the sprawling village of Tattertown.

Sprawled across the countryside, like an old man sleeping on a wicker-weave couch, were the many houses of Tattertown. Some were big and some were small, from the stout well-built houses along the banks of the River Why to the shacks and shanties in Humble Hollow.

Of all the houses that had been built in and around Tattertown, none was bigger than the old Parsnip Palace. Sitting atop a hill overlooking the town, the house had been built years and years before by Potter Parsnip and his wife Paula who filled it with children, laughter and song. For years and years, neighbors listened to the scuffing of feet on hardwood floors as Potter, Paula and the young Parsnips danced about the palace.

But that was years ago. Now old Parsnip Palace had fallen on hard times. The windows were nailed shut and boarded over with plank and nails. Everything was in need of repair.

Living here all alone was the granddaughter of Potter and Paula, Pricilla Parsnip. A mystery to all who met her, she was a secretive, odd otter who dressed in clothes made of old flour sacks stitched with cornsilk bindings.

If the old place was odd on the outside, what was inside made it odder still. For, you see, Pricilla was a finder and a saver of all things discarded or sold beneath value. There were stacks and stacks of well-worn blankets and quilts, and cans of this and that. There were bits of paper and cardboard stacked by size and type. There were rolls and rolls of twine and string.

Late at night Pricilla's flour sack skirts rustled as she moved amongst the stacks of things she had found on the streets that day. She was looking for something - something misplaced, something lost. As her worn slippers shuffled on wooden floors she would mutter over and over, "I open my eyes and look around; I look and look but it can't be found!"

Worse than that, she didn't have the slightest idea what she was looking for!

Her everyday was spent wandering the streets of Tattertown and sometimes in the countryside beyond picking up a bit of this and a bit of that in hopes that this or that was what she was looking for. But, it never was.

Fiddler, Ira Wordworthy, and even old Wandel Wedgie often offered to help her, but to their offers she would always answer the same, "I open my eyes and look around; I look and look but it is never found. Do you know what I am looking for?"

And the answer she got from the folks in town was always the same: a shake of the head followed by a 'Tsk!' Tsk!' 'Tsk!'

"Poor, old Miss Parsnip," they would cluck as she wandered on her way.

But if the truth be known she was far from poor, she was simply very confused.

Now in late summer the rains came to Barely There and moistened the land, long parched by summer's dry and brittle winds. Barren, dried clods of poor earth were enriched by the wealth of these late summer rains. This year was wealthier than most as the storms tried to drown the sorrow of seasons past.

As lightening flashed and thunder echoed mightily from the Mountains of Kota Kazoo, the folk of Barely There rushed quickly from shelter to shelter.

Even Pricilla ran instead of walked, holding a
newspaper above her head.

Like in all things, a little can soon become
a lot. Swollen by the rains, creeks became
rivers that quickly overflowed the banks, dikes
and levies.

It was a flood; frightful to behold!

At first the waters simply oozed over the
banks, covering the land like cool syrup over
hot cakes. But too soon the water raged
through the lowlands and everyone was
caught in the flood!

Like all things the storm soon past and neighbor began helping neighbor clean up the mess. Some were not as fortunate as others. Down in Humble Hollow, Beggary Creek had flooded its narrow banks in a way no one would have expected.

Not one, not two, not even a few of the
rickety homes had survived the flood. Every
single home in Humble Hollow had been
washed away! Even the Hearts, who had built
their shanty on the base of a great stump, had
lost everything. They like others that lived in
the hollow had no clothes, no food, no shelter.

    Barely There is a great place to live and great folks live there. Without pause or question, everyone pitched in to help those in need. Everybody took somebody in and gave them food and shelter.

    But there were far more victims than there were places that they could stay.

    Finally a meeting was called at the Mercantile. "These folks need shelter," old Ira said as everyone gathered around. "What are we to do?"

Fiddler, who had traveled the many miles
from his cabin on Mirror Lake to help those in
need was quick with an answer. "The only place
with space is the old Parsnip Palace up on the
hill. May chance Pricilla will take these folks
in." With that he sloshed up the path to the
Parsnip place.

With muddy footprints left on the weathered wood of the porch, Fiddler rapped on the door. After a time there came the rattling of locks and the skreeching of rusted hinges as the door slowly opened. Cautiously,Pricilla stepped outside.

"Miss Parsnip," Fiddler began, hat in hand, "Sorry to bother you, but we desperately need your help. With the flood and all, there are many folks without shelter. We were hoping that you might help by allowing some to stay with you in your home 'til things are set right."

Old Pricilla looked at Fiddler and in her whispery voice said, "I open my eyes and look around. Oh, I look and look, but it can't be found."

She paused, touching furry paw to chin and asked, "If your homeless folk have what I have been searching for, then they are welcome to stay. But they must give it to me on this porch before they can come inside!"

With that she stepped back inside and shut the door.

Fiddler rushed to Wordworthy's and told everyone the good news.

Ira scratched his head, "I don't exactly know if this is good news or bad. For what is the answer to Pricilla's riddle: I look and look but it cannot be found?"

Quickly they began looking about the store for the *thing* that Pricilla had lost.

They found an ivory pin that someone
had lost and a watch and a pencil or two.
Each found item was taken in turn to Pricilla
to which she sadly answered the same, "No,
that is not what I have lost!"

They spent the whole night looking
under and over everything to find that one
something that was the answer to the riddle.
Finally, Fiddler, who had been digging
through an old box of lost and found, looked
up, slapped his thigh, and laughed, "I've got
it! It's not a *what*! It's a *who*!" With that he
gathered everyone around and told them the
answer to Priscilla's mysterious riddle.

The dawn of a new day painted the countryside in an eerie glow as Fiddler, followed by the now-homeless from Humble Hollow, marched up the winding trail to the old house that sat on the hill. Once there, Fiddler rapped loudly upon the door.

As before, the door opened and there stood Pricilla blinking the sleep from her eyes.

She looked at the crowd and in a sleepy voice said, "I open my eyes and look around. I look and look but it can't be found! Do you know what I'm looking for? If so, please be welcome through my door."

First one, then two, then three, then all moved forward and whispered the answer in Pricilla's ear. She smiled warmly at each in turn and then ushered them inside.

What had Pricilla searched for all her life and not found? What had been given to her on the doorstep of her home that changed her forever?

They gave her no gift
No money to lend.
They each simply said,
"Please be my friend."

And friendship is what we all endlessly search for…

…in the Land of Barely There.

Now that you've read this story true, come to web and we'll share with you. There on a site called SakesAlive you'll find all the characters bright and alive. Write them a letter, one or two, and each in turn will write back to you.

My oh my, SakesAlive
characters are living
and here they thrive.
My, oh my, SakesAlive!

www.sakesalive.com